#40

SuAnn and **Kevin Kiser**

The Birthday Thing

pictures by
Yossi Abolafia

Greenwillow Books
NEW YORK

$5

FOR OUR MOTHERS

Watercolor paints and a black pencil were used for the full-color art. The text type is ITC Pacella.

Text copyright © 1989 by SuAnn and Kevin Kiser
Illustrations copyright © 1989 by Yossi Abolafia

Printed in Singapore by Tien Wah Press
First Edition   10   9   8   7   6   5   4   3   2   1

Library of Congress Cataloging-in-Publication Data
Kiser, SuAnn.   The birthday thing.
Summary: Timothy's family "helps" him create a Birthday Thing that turns out to be exactly what his mother needed for her birthday.
[1. Gifts—Fiction.   2. Birthdays—Fiction.
3. Family life—Fiction]   I. Kiser, Kevin.
II. Abolafia, Yossi, ill.   III. Title
PZ7.K6454Bi 1989   [E]   87-38085
ISBN 0-688-07772-3
ISBN 0-688-07773-0 (lib. bdg.)

Timothy wanted to give his mother
a very special birthday present.
Something that no one else could give her.

On the morning of his mother's birthday,
Timothy began to make the Birthday Thing.

While Timothy's mother worked at her desk, Timothy worked in the kitchen. He mixed flour and salt and water together in a big bowl until it became bread dough clay. He kneaded and cut and rolled and shaped a lump of the dough into a Thing.

His sister Linda came into the kitchen.
"What are you making?" she asked.
"I'm making a Birthday Thing for Mother,
  all by myself," said Timothy.

"It looks sort of like a teapot," Linda said, "but it needs a spout."

Linda made a dough spout, and Timothy attached it to the Thing.

"It might be a little bit small for tea," said Linda as she left.

Timothy kneaded and cut and rolled and shaped
some more dough, and made the Thing bigger.

It didn't look like a teapot anymore.

His brother Doug came into the kitchen.
"What are you making?" he asked.
"I'm making a Birthday Thing for Mother,
all by myself," said Timothy.

"It looks sort of like a fruit bowl," Doug said,
"but it needs some handles." Doug made two dough
handles, and Timothy attached them to the Thing.
"It might be a little bit small for fruit," said
Doug as he left.

Timothy kneaded and cut and rolled and shaped
some more dough, and made the Thing bigger.

It didn't look like a fruit bowl anymore.

Timothy's father came into the kitchen
carrying Timothy's baby sister Alison.
"What are you making?" his father asked.
"I'm making a Birthday Thing for Mother,
all by myself," said Timothy.

"It looks sort of like a breakfast tray," his father said,
"but it needs feet." Timothy's father made four dough feet,
and Timothy attached them to the Thing. Alison poked a
finger through one side of the Thing and smiled.
"It might be a little bit small for a whole breakfast,"
said Timothy's father as he and Alison left.

Timothy kneaded and cut and rolled and shaped the rest of the dough, and made the Thing bigger.

It didn't look like a breakfast tray anymore.
But whatever it was, it was finished.

Timothy's father helped him put the Birthday Thing in the oven.

After it had baked and cooled, Timothy painted it blue
and orange, his mother's favorite colors.

When the Birthday Thing was dry, Timothy wrapped it in lots of colored paper and put it on his mother's desk with the other presents.

"Surprise!" Timothy yelled when his mother opened the
Birthday Thing. His mother looked very, very surprised.
"What a beautiful present, Timothy!" she said.
"But what is it?"
"It's a teapot," said Linda.
"It's a fruit bowl," said Doug.
"It's a breakfast tray," said Father.
Alison just smiled.
"It's a Birthday Thing," said Timothy.

"Why, so it is," his mother said.
  She cleared a space on her desk
  for the Birthday Thing.
"And it's just the thing I need."

She hung rubber bands on Linda's spout. She put pens
in one of Doug's handles, and pencils in the other.
She slid a stack of paper beneath the Thing, and the
paper fit perfectly between Father's dough feet.
She put her silver pen in Alison's finger hole, and she
stacked her mail very neatly in the top of the Thing.

Timothy's mother gave him a big hug.
"Thank you very much for the Birthday Thing, Timothy,"
  she said. "It's just exactly right."
"I made it all by myself," Timothy said. "Almost."